BLOOD FOR COMPANY

JACKIE TRUEBLOOD

authorHOUSE®

AuthorHouse™
1663 Liberty Drive
Bloomington, IN 47403
www.authorhouse.com
Phone: 1 (800) 839-8640

Published by AuthorHouse 05/19/2017

ISBN: 978-1-5246-9167-7 (sc)
ISBN: 978-1-5246-9166-0 (e)

CHAPTER ONE

Autumn is definitely upon us. I can smell it in the air, feel it in the crispness of everything around me. The sun has finally tucked itself behind the horizon, leaving a smear of inky blue darkness behind it.

I walk down the gravel driveway to their leir, a dark two story house set back into the woods. It looks innocent enough on the outside; no one would ever guess that lurking behind those stone walls is a group of the most dangerous creatures on Earth.

Once again, I'm lost in a battle with my own thoughts. Every time is the same. He will hold me, touch me, kiss me, for hours if that's what I want, and all for just one small favor. I let him suck my blood. I suppose, to most people, this sounds grotesque, and not worth the ostracism, but vampires are such beautiful creatures that spending any amount of time with one would make even the bitterest old man smile in ecstasy. Even the brutal act of them sucking your blood is somehow amazing. True, it hurts at first, like someone is sticking two dull hot needles into your flesh, but then their venom kicks in and everything goes numb. Suddenly the world doesn't seem like such a horrible place. Where people hurt you, where they lie and fight and cheat to get what they want. Being in the arms of a vampire is a lot like being in love. At that small point in time you are sheltered from the world…. A shiver goes through me that has nothing to do with the cold. Still, I pull my jacket tighter.

I knock on the door and Titus pulls it open with a smirk. "Back again Aria? This is getting pathetic. You do realize he doesn't really love you?"

I know better than to retort his comments, so I push past him into the living room without a word. Magnon is strewn across the couch looking dazed. He must have just feed.

Titus comes up behind me. "It's a wonder he doesn't just run you dry, there must be something about your company. Give me a taste?" He slithers a hand around my waist, almost instantly an ear deafening growl comes from the stairs to my right.

Vampires and humans have lived in peace for a decade using the blood for company trade, but you had to be careful. Once a vampire has chosen to bite you, to have your blood run through them, they have claim on you. They expect you to be loyal, for life. Many humans have been killed because they have been bitten by multiple vampires. For creatures that live in packs, they are oddly territorial. Fortunately for Perrous, he was the only one I had eyes for, and the only vampire I ever expected to bite me.

I shake Titus's hand off of me. A blur shoots down the stairs and shoves Titus sending him flying across the room and crashing against the far wall. Perrous scoops me up and we shoot back up the stairs before I can take another breath. On our way down the hall to his room I notice Annette's door is closed. She must have tricked another poor soul into following her home so she could feed.

Vampires aren't supposed to kill humans, and fortunately the majority like our deal better than the old ways of hunting. Still, there were some, like Annette who had been around for so long that change wasn't really an option.

Perrous takes me to his room, he strips me down to my underwear, kissing my bare skin softly as he does so. He places me on his bed, then lays down next to me.

"You're back so soon." He runs a finger over the still risen fang marks from my last visit. Two perfectly round red spots on my left shoulder. "I can't say I'm disappointed."

"As unhealthy as this relationship is we do need each other." I mutter.

"I don't think it's unhealthy at all. Sex is the most natural and instinctual need humans have. As is blood lust for vampires." He looks at me for a long moment. For that moment his brown eyes are so filled with pain I can't bare to look into them. Vampires have this nasty habit of projecting what you feel back at you, it is a way to gain your trust. To make you believe they are just like you.

"Perrous, of course I need you." I brush my fingertips over his icy lips. "I'll always need you." I admit sadly.

He takes my hand in his, tracing kisses from my wrist to my elbow and back. "You're so beautiful Aria, I wish I could help you to see how much I need you in return."

I watch him put his lips to my skin. He has to say these things in order for me to believe that his part of the deal has been upheld. I know this. I know he doesn't mean it, but I choose to let myself, for now, believe that he does. I allow myself to believe he wants me because I'm me. I let him kiss me, let him run his hands over me, let him tell me he loves me. In the end I feel better. If only for a short time, it creates relief from the pain. He pulls my wrist toward his mouth, I let out a small shiver as his freezing breath travels down my arm. He bites down and the pain nearly makes me bite through my bottom lip. Just as soon as the pain becomes unbearable, it stops all together. A warmth spreads through me and then, numbness. Not a single thought or feeling. Utter peace.

"You are safe with me Aria. I'll never let anything happen to you." He whispers in my ear before I sink into blackness.

When I come to everything comes at me in waves. I sit up too fast and almost pass out again. My head spinning I turn to look at Perrous. He's still out, will be for awhile by the looks of it. After vampires feed they go into a kind of hyper sleep that lasts for about an hour depending on how much blood they consume. As I understand it, it is the only time they ever rest. Perrous always looks so peaceful, all the lines of his hard face smoothed out. His body completely motionless. I reach out to touch the contours of his bare chest but realize I'm shaking. I look to the open window. Perrous always leaves it open, since he doesn't need to regulate a body temperature he says the cold keeps him sharp. I stand up only to realize just how cold I am. I'm physically shaking from head to foot. I can barely get the window closed my fingers are so numb. I get back into the bed and wrap all of the covers around me. Soon I am fast asleep.

Hours later I awake to find Perrous is gone. I shouldn't be surprised he never stays through the night, but that doesn't make the sting of his absence any easier to bare.

I get up and get dressed monotonously. My right arm is weak and stiff from the bite. I walk into the living room to find it empty, and wonder carelessly where everyone is. Mostly I'm relieved I won't have to be heckled on my way out. My walk home is slow and silent in the early morning light. It's a beautiful fall day. The leaves have just begun to change, the red eating through the green like fire.

I walk slowly up the steps to my apartment, and I push open the door. Hadley is there, arms folded tightly across her chest.

"Where were you?" She already knows, she just wants to hear me say it. She also knows I won't.

"Out..." I reply.

"All night?" She is eyeing me carefully, I must look worse than I think I do. Giving blood takes a lot out of a person.

"Hadley, don't." I take my coat off and throw it carelessly over the arm of our couch.

"You were with him again, I know it. I can smell him on you." She makes that face like I'm covered in raw sewage.

"Well, what do you care who I hang out with?"

"I'm worried about you Aria. I don't like this, it's unhealthy what he does to you. He's a drug to you Aria, you're addicted."

"It's not your job to worry about me." I mutter.

"I'm your sister." She says quietly. "It's in the job description." She takes a breath still eyeing me. "Listen, I know you've been through a lot, but-"

"You have no idea what I've been through." I cut her off bitterly.

"We've all got our shit okay?" She's trying to stay calm.

"Yea? And you deal with yours by drinking. How is that any different?" I snap.

"It's completely different, I drink on the weekends after working all week to wind down and relax. I don't let it disrupt my life or abuse it like you do. I mean this is some sick masochistic shit you're in Aria. I just don't understand." She shakes her head.

Exactly, she has no idea. She can't understand.

She huffs a breath at me then goes to sit on the couch. "Will you just… The next time you want to go there tell me, and we'll find something else to do. Okay? I will show you you don't need that, or him."

I agree because I'm exhausted, because I want this conversation to end. Hadley acts as if by telling me all of this I'll have some kind of revelation, but it's the same conversation I have in my head every time I think about Perrous.

CHAPTER TWO

My week goes by in a haze. Work and sleep, I hardly remember to eat. Nothing seems to be able to pull my mind out of this dream like fog. Then the itching comes crawling back into my skin. Like there is an electrical charge running over the surface of my body. Thursday night's sleep is plagued with images of Perrous, and when I wake I can hardly believe the date. Friday already. It's been 5 days since I've seen Perrous. The longest I have ever gone. The scar on my wrist has vanished like it never happened. I'm starting to crave the numbness again.

I walk into the kitchen where Hadley is making coffee. We are awkwardly silent, but I can see her thoughts play across her face. She is thinking of asking me something but choosing her words.

"So…" She finally says. "Plans tonight?"

"No." I say simply. It's the truth, I plan to come home after work and fall right into my bed where I'll toss and turn before finally falling into what I can only pray to be a dreamless sleep, but of course, she doesn't believe me.

"How about we go out then?"

That sounds arduous. "Sure." I give a weak smile.

I make a deal with myself. If I go out with Hadley tonight, just make it through a couple of hours with her, then I can see Perrous. If I get her drunk enough and take her home she won't even notice I'm gone. Five days. I deserve to see him.

"Great." She actually smiles. "We'll find some place low key and just drink till we get bored."

That's what she says will happen, but really I'll wind up watching some douche bag hit on her all night while I sip drinks by myself. I usually end up small talking with the bartender while they make out. Then he'll use his 'best moves' to try to get her to come home with him. By the end of the night we'll be binging on burgers and pass out in front of the T.V. only to wake up with no recollection of how we got home and a serious hangover.

"That could be fun." I pour myself some coffee. Something tells me I'll be needing massive amounts of caffeine to get through the next 24 hours.

"It'll be good for you, to get out. Have a reason to get dressed up."

That's her nice way of saying I look like shit and should really snap out of it.

"Okay?" She asks, so I nod. Really nothing could make me feel worse at this point, and maybe she is right, maybe going out will be good for the both of us.

"I'll see you after work." I say then down my cup of coffee before walking out the door.

I work as a hostess at one of those bar and grills downtown. Nothing ridiculously fancy or awe inspiring but it keeps me busy and brings in money for rent. My entire day is spent standing with people having a huge smile plastered on my face. A lot of acting goes into my day. Pretending to be pleasant when all you want to do is scream at someone.

My day, as usual, drags on. I've trained myself not to look at the clock. It helps to be surprised when the day is finally over. Patrick, the restaurant manager calls me into his office when my shift is finished. I assume he's going to yell at me for favoring one of the waitresses sections like he always does, so I'm a little taken aback when he says, "Good job this month Aria."

"Oh... Thank you." I reply awkwardly. I never know what to do when someone is complimenting me, so I just stand there smiling blankly like a twit.

"Cali is leaving to have her baby next week. I was wondering if you would like to take over as lead while she is on maternity leave."

"Sure, of course I would." I never understood how head of the wait staff is higher up than hostess, but I'd take the pay raise. Really it only meant I was in charge of the others schedules. Nothing I couldn't handle.

My feet drag on the walk back home. I am so extremely tired, so tempted to fall into my bed and sink into sleep. Unfortunately I'm not that lucky. Even if Hadley wasn't on her way home expecting me to be ready. Even if I could lay down and close my eyes, my mind wouldn't allow sleep to come. Even just being alone now was bringing on bad thoughts. My longing to see Perrous was getting deeper by the day. It had sunk into my bones, a physical aching to be near him again. I shake my head to dislodge my thoughts. I had to decide what to wear, which could take all night in and of itself.

When Hadley walks through the door I'm still hiding in my closet. Literally every shirt I own has been ripped from the hanger and now lay on the floor at my feet.

"Well don't you look pretty." Hadley says from the doorway. "But I don't think you can get away with only wearing underwear, even if it is Seattle."

I scowl at her. "Everything I own is ugly."

"Don't be over dramatic Aria, I'll let you borrow my black dress. You always wanted to wear it out."

"Fine." I mutter. She only offers so I won't have a reason to stay home. Still I'm grateful.

Once we are both dressed, and our lungs are so coated with hairspray it's a miracle we can still breath, we head out the door. It's a long way down the hill from Queen Ann but worth the walk. Hadley is complaining about her outfit the whole way. "I should have worn the red shoes." She keeps saying.

"Hadley, trust me, you look great." I keep assuring her to keep her quiet. Of course she looks gorgeous as always. Leaving me looking like the average bum as usual. Hadley and I have never looked anything close to sisters. The only thing we have in common is our height. Both barely pushing five foot one. She is tiny and blonde with the perfect amount of curves. I on the other hand am brunette and far too skinny. One light and happy, one dark and bitter. It only makes sense that I was the one who ended up with a Vampire. Hadley is the one with a soul, not me.

We get to the bar and of course Hadley is all cheer. The bouncer asks for my I.D. and I scoff at him. Twenty-Five and I'm still getting carded at the same bar we've been going to since we were 19.

"Hey!" The bartender calls us over. "Haven't seen you in forever Aria."

I nod. "I've been mainstreaming." I reply sarcastically.

"How about a drink on the house then?" He smiles.

"Vodka cranberry." Hadley beams at him. She is already scanning the crowd for boys worthy of her attention.

The bartender, I can't remember his name for the life of me, turns to me. "And you love?"

"Just give me something with tons of red bull."

He goes off to make our drinks. Great Hadley is making eyes at some boy and he's on his way over.

The bartender returns with our drinks, and I down mine too quickly. It makes me light headed, but relaxed.

I'm nodding absently as the bartender goes on about life outside his job.

"Oh my God." Hadley says suddenly.

"What?" I ask alarmed.

"That guy is just staring at you..." She hisses.

I turn my head casually and flick my eyes over to where she is looking. She's right, a man with bright green eyes and a mess of auburn hair is staring straight at me, so intensely it makes me blush suddenly and turn away.

"Do you know him or something?" The bartender asks.

I shake my head. I have never seen him before in my life, yet something about his presence seems familiar. Then it hits me. The color drains from my face. He must be an anti-vampire activist, and somehow he knows I've been with one. That I've sacrificed my soul to the undead. I don't look back, but I can still feel him staring at me. My breath becomes shallow and uneven.

"Aria?" Hadley's voice makes me jump. "Are you okay?"

I give a minute nod. "I need air." I'm not even sure if she hears me, but I have to get out. The air is too warm it feels like liquid pooling into my lungs, and I can't catch my breath. I push past several people to reach the door. The air out here isn't any better thanks to the horde of smokers crowding the exit. So I walk around the side of the building, lean against the stone wall, and inhale until it feels like my lungs might burst. Just when I think I've gotten my nerves under control, a noise comes from the shadows.

"Hello?" I call, but of course there is no answer. I've seen enough scary movies to know where this is headed, so I pick up a rock to defend myself.

Then he walks into the light. His green eyes set ablaze by the moonlight. "Hey" He grins casually.

For a moment I'm so dazed I can't even think straight.

"Sorry, I didn't mean to scare you." He glances at the rock in my hand, and my grip tightens around it. I may not be getting the killer vibe from him at the moment, but I can't forget the first impression he's made.

"How did you do that?" I ask still dazed by the intensity of his eyes.

"Do what?" He smirks sending a chill through me.

Why does he seem so familiar? "I saw you. One second you're in the bar and the next you're hiding down an alleyway."

He flashes a smile that nearly knocks me over. "Guess you don't know too many vampires that go out in public."

"You're a…. Oh." Suddenly it all makes sense.

"James." He replies.

"Right." I smile dumbly.

"And you are?"

"Um…" I look around suddenly aware of how alone we are. "Aria."

"Aria." He repeats. The word sounds like music on his lips. "Come on, I want to show you something."

I look around, there is no way out of this. And as messed up as it is, now that I know what he is, he doesn't seem that dangerous. I drop the rock, and we both stand there as the echoes of it's fall fills the space around us. He turns and quickly bounds towards the wall opposite us. In one catlike jump he hurls himself up onto a metal fire escape. He leans over holding his hand out to me. This simple gesture shocks me. I've never known a vampire to be polite. "What are you?" I ask once again dazed by him.

"I'll show you." His smile is brilliant white even in the dingy light being cast over us by street lamps.

I don't know what compels me to grab his hand, I should be running, any sane person would be miles away from this situation by now, but I do. He pulls me up as if he were tugging on the string of a balloon. Then we are running up the iron steps to the roof. A feeling builds in my chest so strong I think for a second I'm going to throw up, but when I finally let it out I'm laughing. Big, strong, full body laughs.

"I can't remember the last time I laughed." I admit to James clutching at my chest.

He laughs too. "Well, you should more often, you're very good at it." He says.

We walk over and sit on the ledge of the building. The sky is perfectly clear, the air filled with the sounds of distant laughter. I study James's face for a long moment. He is so still he could be made of glass. "You are unlike any vampire I have ever met." I say. "I almost don't believe you are."

His face turns dark. "Believe it." He turns his fangs to the light to show me. "More than anything I wish I wasn't, but this is what I am."

"What makes you so... different?" I realize I'm being incredibly invasive, but I can't help myself. He is absolutely captivating.

"Most vampires choose to live in packs, but this makes us more inhuman, hostile, and unbelievably competitive. So I choose to live alone, and to interact with humans as much as possible."

I nod. "I've been around the nest in Seattle a lot. Inhuman does not even begin to describe them."

"You've been with one." He's not asking, he knows.

"How?" I stare at him dumbly. Of course he knows, why else would he have been so drawn to me in the bar.

"Fang marks never really disappear to our eyes."

The color leaves my face in an instant. Suddenly I feel naked and so ashamed I want to cry. I can feel every mark on my body as if they were new. My arms, my neck, my bare back littered with with at least a hundred bites.

"It's odd, usually a vampire will only bite their mate in the same few places. It's almost like-"

"Like he didn't care for me at all." I finish staring at the dark pavement.

"No, on the contrary, I think he cared for you a great deal. Marking you the way he did is a highly territorial gesture. It's like he is challenging any other vampire to even look at you." He scans my face. "He must be worried you'll break the treaty. That you'll leave him."

My eyes are still glued to the pavement. "What you must think of me." I shake my head. "How I must look to you…" I can't meet his eyes. I want nothing more in this moment than to be invisible.

"I don't think badly of you." He says. "If anything I understand better than most. You must love him."

"No." I finally look at him again. "No, what Perrous and I had was never love."

"Had?" He asks making me blush again.

"Yes, I've decided toxic relationships aren't really my thing." I sigh thinking of Hadley downstairs with some random guy.

"What?" He inquires.

"I should go back inside. Hadley is probably throwing a fit because she's too drunk and the bartender won't let her leave to look for me.

He nods slowly thinking to himself.

We walk back down the fire escape. He then lifts me over the edge and sets me down on the concrete. He follows me down by throwing himself over the edge to land next to me without a sound. "Show off." I tease.

He stands there looking me over for a second. "As to how you look to me," He breaths, "I don't think you could ever be anything but beautiful." He takes his hand and lifts my chin toward the light. "Actually, in this light your bites look stunning, almost as if they are glowing." He traces a finger down my collar bone, leaving little goose bumps on my skin. He takes his hand back.

I smile because he's ridiculous, but I want him to be right. "Goodnight James."

I turn to walk away.

"Goodnight Aria." His voice is just a whisper, and when I turn back to smile at him, he has vanished.

CHAPTER THREE

"Aria Candace Hawkins!" Hadley is slurring already. "Where the fuck were you?" She yells at me. "You disappeared for 20 minutes! I wanted to look for you but *Sean* wouldn't let me." She glares in the bartenders direction. I knew his name was something simple, forgettable.

"I met someone." I say

"Really!" She squeals putting her arm around me, leading us back to our seats at the bar, suddenly forgiving. "You like him? Is he coming in?" She looks toward the door.

"Yes, I do like him." I smile. "But no, he left."

Sean hands us more drinks and tries to give me a coy smile.

"I met someone too." Hadley beams.

"I bet you did." I mutter before taking a drink.

"His name is Ryan, he's in a band."

"Jesus Hadley, can't you have a little variety?"

She scowls at me then turns to the bartender. "Will you get Aria another drink please? She's being square."

Sean nods to the drink in my hand so I smile absently and take another sip.

I don't remember much after that. Random babbling to Ryan and his friends. Then suddenly Hadley and I are home laughing hysterically because she can't make it up the stairs in her heels.

I wake up the next morning face down on my bed still wearing all my clothes from the night, the pendant from my necklace jabbing into my throat. Hadley is drooling on the pillow next to me. I sit up and the headache hits me all at once. I stand up to head to the bathroom and step on something sharp. I look down to see a broken plate. "Bitch." I mutter at Hadley, she is always breaking shit when she's drunk. As if in response she groans and rolls onto her back. I take another step to avoid the broken plate. The motion makes me so nauseous I have to run to the toilet. How can Hadley do this every weekend? I felt like death and it was only Saturday morning.

When I'm finally able, I head back to bed to lay my head on the pillow in defeat.

Hadley turns her head to look at me. Her eye makeup is smeared down her cheek. "Do you miss him?" She whispers after a minute.

"Every day." I whisper back.

"And Perrous?"

"Don't." I say feeling nauseous again.

She hesitates. "Did you love him?"

"No, not really."

"And you're done with him right?"

I nod then put my hand on her upturned cheek. "Thank you. Even if I want to die right now, I did have fun."

"I know Tequila," She says "never again..." She groans and we laugh.

Monday morning comes too quickly. I arrive at work and immediately head to Patrick's office to hand in the girls schedules for the next two weeks.

"Are you alright you look tired?" Is the first thing out of his mouth.

Thanks asshole. "No, I'm fine." I reply

"Are you sure? I hope I didn't throw too much at you at once."

"I just have a headache, that's all. Trust me, I can handle being lead."

"Okay." He smiles. "Then get to it."

The day is painfully slow and seems endless. As soon as it gets dark I'm so relieved I could cry, I get to go home soon.

I'm on my way to a table with a tray full of food when Kathryn stops me. "I think a vampire just came in." she nearly giggles with excitement. "They're in your section." She winks.

My heart drops into my stomach. My head swirls but I force myself to take a breath and walk over to my table to serve out their dishes. A million thoughts are running through my head. What if it's Perrous or someone from the nest? What will I say? How do I explain my sudden absence? Worse, what if it's Annette here to end me in front of the entire restaurant. A cold chill runs down my spine. She always has been one for dramatics. I swallow the acid clinging to the back of my throat, and force a smile onto my face. "Can I get you anything else this evening?" My voice is surprisingly clear I feel like I'm shouting. The family doesn't seem to notice, they dive right into their food without giving me another glance. "Enjoy." I manage before turning to glance at all the tables in my section. My heart stutters as my eyes lock onto the lone vampire sitting by the row of window. James. Staring out at the darkened streets he looks like a statue carved out of pure pale marble. I walk toward him slowly watching his stillness and amazed by his perfection. He turns his head, suddenly flicking his eyes to mine. A smile creeps over his face obviously amused by my expression.

"What are you doing here?" I squeak out.

"I was hungry." He chuckles. "Were you spying on me?"

My whole body feels like it's on fire. "What?"

"Just now, you were spying on me."

"No." I demand.

"I never meet a spy before." His smile widens.

"Are you finished?" I mock glare at him.

The glimpse I get from his perfect white fangs makes the hair on my arms prickle.

"It's okay if you were you know. It happens to the best of us." He is searching my face for something.

I roll my eyes. "I'm sure everyone finds you captivating." I can't believe how easy it is to joke with him, a vampire. I'm more messed up than I thought.

He looks at me innocently as if he has no idea the effect he has on humans. "And what about you?"

I make a face. "What about me?"

"Do you find me captivating?" He flashes that cunning smile at me again.

"Unfortunately." I admit looking down at the menu in his hands.

Again I feel his gaze searching my face. "Can I see you sometime?"

"You're seeing me now." I joke. It's hard to turn off.

"I mean, can we go out?" He corrects, his mouth forming oddly over the words.

He's looking at me so expectantly I have to look away before I can reply. "James." His name croaks out. I lick my lips suddenly aware of how thirsty I am. "I don't think that's a very good idea."

"Why?'

I still can't look at him. "Because." Because I don't want to die...

"'Because' is the beginning of a sentence, Aria, not a reason."

"Because if Perrous found out he would kill us both. Hell, I thought it was Perrous or Annette here tonight when Kathryn told me a vampire was just sitting in our restaurant." I'm starting to get nervous. I swear I just saw something flash under that street lamp.

"Annette." He exclaims surprised. He looks me over for a long moment, and I pray he doesn't see that I'm sweating. God, it's hot in here, and why am I so damn thirsty? "You are still with him? Perrous?"

"No." I say firmly.

"Then what is the problem? I'm not cute enough?"

I choke out a laugh. Calling him 'cute' is like comparing the brightness of the sun to a candle flame. "That's not fair..."

"Right." He still has a huge grin on his face.

"Are you going to order, or are you just going to sit there?" I somehow manage to get the lightness back into my voice.

"There is not a whole lot for me on this menu. Unless you can drain a few raw steaks into a wine glass for me." He winks.

I stare at him blankly for a moment. I know he's joking but I have to get away from him for a minute so I can find my head again. "I'll see what I can do." I turn to walk away.

"Aria." His cold hand brushes my arm making me turn back. "I'm sorry." He says. "I'm not trying to make this difficult for you. I just…" Now he's the one looking nervous. "There's something about you. I can't seem to get you out of my head."

I watch him for a long moment. The truth is I haven't stopped thinking about him since that night at the bar, and instead of Perrous I've been seeing his face in my dreams. I wish more than anything that I didn't feel for him. That I could be cold and just tell him to get lost. Then the dilemma could be over and I could deal with Perrous and Annette's wrath on my own. How pathetic that I want him to protect me, that I believe he can. No one can help me. I am damaged beyond repair. And looking at his perfect face I realize something… I am so fucked.

"I'm off at 8." I say before running to go hide in the kitchen.

CHAPTER FOUR

We walk down the street as if we are old friends reunited. Once again I'm blown away by how comfortable we are together.

"So." He says slowly after a pause. "Can I ask you something?"

This is never good. I hesitate, then nod, realizing there is no point in hiding things from him.

"Why are you so… guarded?" He says the word as if it's made of glass.

"What do you mean?"

He fidgets with the sleeve of his jacket. "I guess I'm trying to ask why you got involved with Perrous. How you've become the… way you are." He says carefully.

I stop to look at him straight on. "Do you really want to know?"

"Of course."

"If I tell you, you have to tell me your story too."

He nods so we sit on a bench facing the park.

I sigh pushing the toe of my shoe into the dirt. "I'm warning you now, I come with a lot of baggage. So, I'm going to ask again. Are you sure you want to hear it? You want to know everything?"

"Yes." He says blatantly. So unafraid of me.

I take a breath and blow it out threw my lips. I've never had to tell this story to a vampire before. "When I was in high school things were perfect, I mean I wasn't gorgeous or popular or anything, but I was a good student, had a great family, and I had a boyfriend who was my everything, my soulmate. The first boy I ever loved. I was happy."

He's looking me over, trying to read the emotion on my face. "So what happened?"

"He died." I reply. "Suicide."

James is silent.

"His parents made it out to be an accident. It was dark and raining, but I knew him. Always careful." I breath. "Either way he hit the side of the 520 bridge at full speed, right at the point where the railing drops down far enough that the car went right threw it. He died on impact."

James shakes his head.

"Half of me died that day with him."

"That is… so awful, Aria."

"At first I was just angry. Angry at him, angry at myself."

He is still shaking his head slowly.

"And… It gets better, two weeks after the 'accident' I found out I was pregnant."

He looks at me blankly. "You have a kid?"

I look away from him, his eyes are too heavy I can't bare the weight. "No, I don't."

He is silent for a moment, looking off into the trees as if they can clarify his questions.

"After I was angry I was bitter. Then the depression took hold of me. My parents checked me into a psychiatric hospital. One of the many reasons we are not on speaking terms."

James is still silent, still looking away from me. I knew he didn't want to hear this. No one ever does.

"When they finally decided I wasn't a danger to myself they let me live with Hadley, my sister." I swallow, for some reason I can't stop talking. "Perrous was my way to... numb the pain."

His head finally swivels back in my direction. "I could tell... When I first saw you. You are beautiful Aria, but... there was only stillness behind your eyes. Like you were shutting everything out." He is searching my face. "But," His mouth ticks into a smile. "Then you looked at me, so curious instead of afraid, and you laughed with me." He beams making heat pool in my cheeks. "There was some kind of ignition in you when we met. You haven't been the same since." He winks.

I roll my eyes.

He takes my hand, suddenly serious again. "Perrous may have been a drug for you, but maybe I can be a cure." He runs a hand along my jawline, then very slowly traces my lips with one cold finger. He leans in and briefly touches his frozen lips against mine.

I want so badly to tell him that I don't need him. To release him from my burden. "I want to believe that I could survive without you, but I'm afraid we've reached the point of no return."

"From the second I saw you I knew there was no going back." He flashes that magnificent smile and kisses me again.

I stand, pulling him with me. "Come on. Hadley will be worried."

We stop at the bottom of the stairs to my apartment and he surprises me by leaning in suddenly toward my throat, for a second I'm convinced my heart actually stops, but he only grabs the ends of my scarf and wraps it tighter around me, and I swear he is toying with me because the smile playing on his lips is very mischievous. He is still leaning in. I can smell his skin and feel the chill coming off of his hands as they linger only centimeters from my face. He kisses me lightly before saying "Goodnight Aria."

His lingering scent is still making my head spin. I look up to see Hadley suddenly duck behind the window curtain. Great, this is a fight I don't think I can handle right now. I walk slowly up the steps and push the door open. Hadley is busying herself in the kitchen.

"Did your shift run late?" She calls.

"No." I reply. Maybe if I come clean right away she won't start a fight and I can finally lay down.

"I thought I heard voices." She comments. "Who were you with?"

I set my bag down. "Uh…" My mouth suddenly goes dry. She must sense as much because she begins pouring me a glass of wine. "Remember that guy I met outside the bar the other night?"

To my surprise her face actually lights up. "Oh! That was him? He's cute."

"Cute?" I question taken aback. Then it hits me. There is no way she knows he is a vampire.

"I mean, he *sounded* cute." She shrugs misinterpreting my tone.

She hands me the glass so I take a drink, then raise an eyebrow at her. "Hadley, I know you saw us."

She shrugs again. "I was curious." She walks over to sit on the couch so I follow. "Tell me about him."

I fiddle with my glass. "He's… Different."

"Well, the last normal guy you dated was years ago, Aria."

I swallow. "That's not *really* what I meant by different."

She narrows her eyes at me. "Okay, what did you mean?" She's giving me the benefit of the doubt.

I hate to disappoint her but if I lie about it now it will only make things worse later. "He *is* a vampire."

She sighs rubbing her temple. "Aria…"

"But he is also different. I mean you saw him, he doesn't even look like a vampire. He's unlike any person I've ever met Hadley, living or…. other." I try to crack a smile.

"I just don't understand why you do this to yourself Aria."

"It's not like I seek these guys out… And it's different this time, James actually wants to *date* me. We haven't even talked about the blood sucking thing."

"Cause it's only the root of what he is."

I shake my head. "I don't think it is." Strangely this hadn't occurred to me until I said it. "The way he talks Hadley," I shake my head again. "It's like he wishes he wasn't a vampire. He tries to stay away from everything that makes him inhuman."

Hadley sighs taking another long sip from her glass.

"Just meet him, you'll see what I mean."

CHAPTER FIVE

The days are getting shorter and colder. The once brilliant orange trees now stand naked against the dark sky. James and I walk slowly up the hill to my apartment, his cold fingers intertwined with mine. The bite in the air has made my exposed hand go numb, but I won't dare remove it from his.

"Honestly, no one else has answered these questions for you? Common sense, the internet?" James says.

"Just humor me, okay?"

"Alright," He sighs, "fire away."

"Sleeping in coffins?"

He looks sideways at me. "Don't be absurd, Aria. You know very well that is a myth. Vampires do not need sleep."

"But you do rest, after you feed right?"

"Right, but it's not *sleep*, it's more of a short hibernation." He replies.

"Okay, no coffins then. How about the sun?"

"What about the sun?"

"If you go out during the day do you burst into flame?" I look out toward the dark horizon.

"Only direct sunlight. We can go out in overcast and be fine, that's why I like Washington so much." He smiles down at me.

"But otherwise, only at night?"

"Vampires are creatures of the night, Aria. Most vampires only come out at night because that's their advantage. We are made for the night, created for the hunt. We are born out of darkness."

I look up to see his eyebrows pinched.

"Which leads to my next question…" I swallow, looking down at my shoes. "How do you make a vampire?"

He doesn't answer, so I look back up at him. He looks stoic, lost in thought.

"I mean, obviously it's not through a bite or I'd turned a hundred times over." I try to laugh to get him back to answering my questions but it comes out halfharted. We are only one house away from my complex, I don't want our time together to end, not like this. I tug on his hand, he looks down at me in surprise, as if he is just realizing I've been standing next to him this whole time.

"That's enough questions for today I think." He finally smiles again. "Besides we are here." He nods towards the steps to my home. My heart sinks. I don't want to be without him.

He lets go of my hand, sending a twinge of panic through me. He pushes my hair back in one swift motion, leaving his hand on my skin. The cold makes the hair on the back of my neck stand on end. He pulls me into him kissing me firmly. When we part I have to force myself to remember how to breath. "May I come up?" He asks, his lips still inches from mine.

My heart races. Up... into my dingy apartment. Hadleys face flashes into my mind making my stomach clench uncomfortably.

"Hadley is home." I say staring up at one of the illuminated windows.

"You haven't mentioned me?"

"Uh, I have..." I swallow. "I just don't think *now* is the best time for her to meet my... Vampire."

James suppresses a grin. "Well, then can I take you out tomorrow?"

"Out?" I ask slowly.

"Yes, I believe dinner is customary."

"*You* want to take me to dinner?" I smile. "Will it involve me drinking blood?"

He rolls his eyes. "I was thinking the Italian place on Virginia."

"I don't think they serve blood." My smile grows.

"Aria." He scolds gently.

"So, what, you're just going to sit there and watch me eat?"

He nods. "I like watching you do human things."

I stare at him for a long moment. "You're serious?"

"As the grave."

"James..."

"Humor me, Aria." He gives me a sly smile.

"Fine." I say reaching up to touch his face. I kiss him slowly, then turn to run up the stairs.

Once again I stand in my closet, unhappy with any clothing purchase I've made in the past few years. "He'll be here any minute." Hadley says walking into the room.

"Helping or hindering." I mutter.

"You look good in that." She nods to the clothes I have on. A nice button up blue shirt, and skinny jeans.

I tug on my shirt. "Blue is a weird color on me."

Hadley rolls her eyes.

"Plus, this just doesn't feel… nice enough for a date." I frown down at my outfit.

"So wear a dress." She reaches for a cap sleeved emerald green dress that I haven't worn since high school. "Just try it on, if it sucks you can go back to the blue."

She watches as I remove the blouse and jeans, then tug the dress over my head. She is right, it's better than the blue, still, I can't help but to feel self conscious.

The doorbell rings making my stomach do a summersault.

"I'll get it." Hadley says as I shoot around the corner into the bathroom.

Quickly, I run a comb through my ratty hair, and apply a thick layer of mascara. I take one last look in the mirror. He already likes you, I remind myself, though it doesn't calm my nerves.

I enter the living room to find Hadley and James standing awkwardly. His green eyes turn bright at the sight of me.

"Aria." He smiles, "As always, you look beautiful."

Heat rushes to my face. "Thank you."

Another beat of awkward silence.

"I've made reservations, we should leave."

I nod and grab a coat before we walk out the door.

"Have fun!" Hadley calls, "You know, just not *too* much fun. No biting on the first date." She blabs. I shoot her a death glare then swing the door closed.

We walk down the stairs. "Your sister is…"

"Obnoxious." Belligerent, downright rude!

"I was going to say, nice, but nothing like you." He grabs my hand as we walk making my heartbeat quicken.

We walk up to a packed restaurant. Immediately I notice the eyes of several people land on the creature next to me. The host walks us to a small round table smack in the center of everyone. I swear I can hear "Vampire" being hissed under the breaths of everyone around us, but as I glance around I notice no one is looking directly at us.

"I'll have the red wine. Aria?" James' voice pulls me back.

"Me too, thanks." I smile awkwardly. I hate being served by others, I feel like I should be helping. Then I notice the waiter, like the rest of the people around us, doesn't make direct eye contact even with me. Sweat beads on the back of my neck. I look up at the ceiling, taking a deep breath. The glass chandelier above us looks as though it's never been cleaned. I wish I could peel back the roof, replace this hot stuffiness with the frigid night air.

"Maybe this was a bad idea." James says eyeing me.

"I'm fine." I reply looking back at him. "It's just warm in here."

Our waiter returns with our wine. I glance down at the menu, everything is wildly overpriced. A pang of guilt goes through me.

"I'll have the chicken."

The waiter finally looks a James. "And you sir?" The edge in his voice makes me cringe, but James only laughs brightly. "Nothing for me, thank you."

The waiter takes our menus and disappears.

"I didn't realize being around people would make you this uncomfortable." He says softly.

"It doesn't." I respond squirming in my seat. "I have some more questions for you." I say to change the subject.

"Alright." He eyes me skeptically.

"And you won't get offended?"

"Very few things offend me anymore, Aria." He smirks making eye contact with a couple at another table who had been staring.

"How do you... make a living." I say carefully.

He smiles to himself. "I inherited my family's land and money."

"Oh." I nod, he's never mentioned his family before.

"And there isn't much a vampire needs to spend money on."

Luckily, it is loud enough in the restaurant that I'm the only one who flinched at his word choice.

"What about... where you live?"

"I live here in Seattle."

"I figured... I meant, how do you live?"

"You're asking me what I feed on."

I swallow feeling anxious again. "I..." the waiter comes with my food. "Thank you."

"What is it that you really want to know Aria?"

"How does someone become... like you?"

"Obviously, you know it's not from just being bitten. A human must drink our blood to become one of us."

"You are what you eat..." I say solemnly.

He chuckles.

I take a bite of the chicken and realize how extremely famished I actually am. I wolf down half the plate before I remember James is just sitting there staring at me with his bright eyes.

"Sorry." I set my fork down scrambling for something else to say.

"Never apologize for being human, Aria." He takes a sip of wine which brings on a whole other round of questions.

"You can eat human food?"

"I can, it doesn't do much for me though." He chuckles again.

"Does alcohol even have an effect on you?"

He shakes his head swirling the glass. "No, but I do enjoy the taste once in awhile." He watches the liquid settle before smiling back at me.

"Did you enjoy it?" He nods to the plate in front of me.

I nod. "Yes, it was delicious." I swallow another drink of wine, suddenly feeling out of place again. "Thank you, for taking me out. I honestly never expected it."

"I wanted to prove to you that I can at least act human for a night."

"You're much too interesting to act like anything."

His smile widens, and I catch a glimpse of his fangs as his lips pull apart.

The waiter interrupts our moment by rudely smacking the check down on the table between us.

"Have a pleasant evening." He says through a fake smile.

James looks at him with defiance. "I'm sorry, Aria, didn't you want dessert?"

I shake my head furiously. "I'm fine."

James flashes his fangs at the waiter. "My mistake." He shrugs casually handing the man his credit card. The waiter returns in record time, and practically pushes us out the door.

James is still smiling. "That was fun."

"You take far too much pleasure in torturing others."

He shoots me a sinful glance. "Vampire."

We start walking, I'm not even sure in a specific direction. A dangerous thought shoots through my mind. "You live close to here?" I say to the sidewalk.

I can practically hear him smirk.

"Yes I do." James takes my hand pulling me closer.

CHAPTER SIX

James puts his hand on my bare back, tracing my spine lightly with his fingertips. I turn my head to look at him. "How can I feel like I know you so well after we've only just met?"

"It's part of vampire nature. You're supposed to feel like you can trust me immediately. It's how we get humans to let us feed."

My heart beats faster. Did he just admit he tricked me into loving him? "Don't you feel the same way about me?"

"Aria..." He says slowly.

A pit opens in my stomach. He has to feel the same way. I won't survive his answer.

"Of course I do. When you spend centuries trying to find someone to share things with you don't hesitate to take a chance."

My heart swells at his words. "Then don't ever doubt my feelings for you."

"It's just hard for me to believe that you..." He looks at the floor. "Would actually want me. Even though, I am who I am."

I sigh. "That seems backwards."

He puts his nose on mine. "Don't ever doubt my feelings for you." He kisses me swiftly before bounding off the bed.

"James." I sit up wrapping the blanket around myself. "When are you going to tell me what happened to you?"

He shoots me a worried look then proceeds to stare darkly at the floor.

"James?" I insist.

"Another time" He snaps.

"You promised me a month ago. I haven't seen Hadley, I'm about to get fired from work because I'm such a zombie when I do go in."

He looks at me suddenly his face full of concern.

"Not to mention we haven't even talked about the very thing that keeps you living. I've spent every possible minute with you since you asked me out that night… But I don't know anything about you."

"Aria-"

"Just tell me one thing?" I plead.

He sighs heavily then plops back down on the edge of the bed.

"What do you want to know?"

"Well," I swallow. He won't answer this one I already know. "You don't feed from me, so who do you feed from?"

He shakes his head. "Something else." His voice is so sharp I don't push it.

"Then tell me how you got like this." I put my hand on his back. It is, despite the heat in the room, as cold as stone and just as hard. "Tell me how you were changed."

His green eyes stare blankly out the window, as if he can see what he's about to tell me being played out on a video screen. "I was just a boy, only 20, when I ran away. I tried to run from everything I knew, from my family, from my fate in that life. I knew our woods like they were my playground, but when I hit the mountains… It was so cold. I knew if I just kept going west I'd eventually hit the water, and I could build my own home, have my own life out there. Finally I could be in charge of my own fate." He stays quiet for a while and I'm afraid that's all he's going to tell me. "I had been wandering around the mountains for two weeks, finally running out of food. I was all but dead when Annette found me, clinging to my last hopeful breath. She saved me, made me stronger as I changed, taught me to hunt, to kill quickly, be a 'good' vampire." He scoffs.

All his words are crashing together, they fire at me like bullets, lodging themselves in my lungs.

"Annette is your creator…" I nearly gag on the words.

He nods unphased by my reaction, which makes my breathing become even more frantic.

"I'm going to ask you something, and don't you dare lie to me." The anger has bloomed into my cheeks. "Do you know Perrous?"

He nods again. Suddenly I feel so betrayed I want to reach out and smack him.

"Did you know when we met that I know Annette?"

He turns to look at me quizzically. "No. Annette's coven is fairly new. Perrous is her latest creation." He sneers. "I was her first."

"Then why aren't you part of her coven?"

"I was at one point. For many decades it was just her and me."

"What happened?" I ask quietly.

"Well, you've seen her, she's insane and highly irrational, even for a vampire. She's old, the oldest vampire I've ever met. Having to live like that for so long, seeing everyone you know and love either die or leave you…" He shakes his head. "It does things to your mind."

"You said her coven in Seattle is new, what happened to the one you were with?"

"After me, she changed four others…" He looks back out the window. "She killed them all."

My heart jumps into my throat and I'm unable to speak.

"When I left she went crazy, completely lost her mind. She used to send me these letters, I have no idea how she would find out where I was, but…" His eyes scrutinize my face. "What?" He finally notices I'm not speaking and my face has turned green with nausea.

"We are so fucked." I manage to choke out "This, is bad, James. This is so bad."

"What are you talking about?"

"At first I thought I betrayed her coven with another vampire, which is a bad enough offence. Since you haven't bitten me I was under the impression it wasn't an extreme situation, but now… Now." I throw the blanket off of me suddenly too hot.

"What are you doing?"

I tung on my jeans, and jam a shirt over my head inside out, I'm not even sure it's mine. "I have to go, I need to get out of here."

"Aria," He grabs me by the shoulders forcing me to stop and look him in the eye.

"She will kill me, James." The reality of my words makes me so afraid all I want to do is stay here, curl into him, and let him protect me, but all I can think about is Hadley. Alone in the same place Annette will expect me to be. Of what she will do if I'm not there, if she found me here with James. I shutter.

"I would never let her."

"James…" I put my hands on either side of his face, and pull his face to mine. "I won't leave Hadley to face my consequences… Please understand."

He nods then kisses me slowly.

Walking out the door is one of the hardest things I have ever done. It physically hurts to be away from him, knowing I may never come back into his embrace again. It feels as if someone has taken a bread knife and severed me in two then separated the halves like velcro.

CHAPTER SEVEN

I open the door to our apartment to find everything is dark. "Hadley?" I call into the empty space. I go to turn on a light but the switch flips with no effect. I run toward her bedroom and whip the door open. "Hadley" I breath with relief. She is laying in bed, a flashlight in her hand reading a book.

The flashlight beam shoots to my face making me squint. "Aria?" She asks sitting up. "What are you doing home?"

"I thought…" What can I tell her? "I hadn't seen you in a while."

"I'm still here." She turns back to her book. "You should get some sleep, you look tired."

"Okay." I try to smile. It's understandable she's upset.

I shut her door and head down the hall to my own room. I don't even bother looking for a flashlight. I go straight to my bed and plop down. The sheets are cold underneath me from lack of use.

"Good evening, Aria."

My heart nearly leaps out of my chest, and I sit bolt upright. Every hair on my body is standing up, my skin crawling with electricity. Annette is staring at me from the shadows across the room.

"You *are* here." I accuse.

"Lucky you showed up when you did, I was starting to get bored." Her dark eyes slide to the door then click back to me.

"What do you want?"

"Your head on a stake." She smirks.

Bile rises up into my throat. I wish I could spit it at her. That it would burn her eyes out.

"But, unfortunately, I promised Perrous I wouldn't kill you, and as he is my newest and most loyal son, I don't want to go against him."

"He told you *not* to kill me?" He must want to kill me for himself. I shutter as a chill rises up my spine.

She scoffs. "Humans really are oblivious." She says almost to herself. "Yes, silly girl. Perrous loves you, he will always love you, blah blah blah."

This notion nearly knocks me back down on the bed. She has to be lying. Perrous and I had an understanding, a symbiotic need for each other. Never love. Why would Annette lie to me about something so trivial to her?

"Vampires shouldn't have the capability to love, but there is always one human, if not properly taken care of, that we can become... overly attached to."

"That's why you always kill your victims."

"Oh honey no, that's just fun." She laughs, and again the urge to spit acid at her rises. "Any human worthy of not killing becomes my family."

"So," I swallow. "If you're not here to kill me, why are you here?"

She contemplates this. Walks over to my dresser and starts thumbing through the jewelry on top of it. "It seems you've developed a taste for my creations Aria." She is overly observant of the angel necklace my mother gave me as a child. "The most recent being my eldest, James."

I don't like the way she says his name, as if she owns it. "What do you want Annette?"

She drops the necklace and glares at me. "I plan to visit James after I leave here. I'm going to tell him if he wishes to avoid my wrath he will leave Seattle and never return."

"And you want me to do the same?"

Her cat like grin widens the malice reaching her eyes. "No, your punishment will be to stay here. To stay as far away from my nest as humanly possible. That includes James."

My heart falls. She's leaving me with just enough to make sure I won't hurl myself off of a building. I couldn't do that to James, even if we aren't together, and I could never do that to Hadley. After everything she's done for the both of us. I'll be forced to stay right here. Forever the same as everything else changes around me.

"If you look for James, or if you even think about crawling back to Perrous, I *will* kill you. No matter what promises I've made, if you cross me again your blood will be mine."

I swallow the hard lump in my throat.

"You will go back to the way life was, without Perrous. Miserable and alone. Do you understand?"

I nod, unable to speak, unable to breath.

In a flash of black Annette vanishes out the door without so much as a creak from the floorboards. For a long moment

I sit in stunned silence. Then the waves of agony begin to break over me. I burry my face in my pillow so Hadley won't hear the sobs. I cry out for James, willing him to be rational. Sleep doesn't come, only my mind wandering off on horrible tangents.

In the morning I'm forced to face Hadley in the kitchen.

"Are you okay?" She says to her coffee.

I take the seat across from her at our dinky table. "Not really." I mumble.

"What's happened?" She scrutinizes my face.

The tears flood up again, hot and unrelenting. "I've ruined everything Hadley." I sob. "How do I always make such a mess of things."

"Aria…" She puts her hand on my arm, a reflex. "You and James broke up?"

I choke out a short laugh. "Something like that…"

"I really am sorry." I can see her trying to find the right thing to say. "I know we fight, but I'm your sister Aria. Don't ever forget you have me."

I nod and mutter, "I know."

It is my day off so I have to say goodbye to Hadley. Suddenly alone again I slump down on the couch to stare at the empty house. There is a pile of bills sitting by the door, neatly stacked already payed and stamped. Thank God for Hadley. I would never survive on my own without her.

To keep my mind off of not seeing James I clean. Scrubbing the floors and counters until my fingers bleed and my nose stings from the chemical smell. I vacuum, I do my laundry, then thinking it will be a nice gesture since I've been neglectful to her, I wander into Hadley's room to grab her dirty clothes. I lean down to pick up the few socks that litter the floor, that's when I spot something underneath her dresser. It's the corner of a picture. The shadow of a familiar smile glares back at me. I reach out and drag the picture toward me only gently touching the edges. It's a picture of a little girl about the age of 4 or 5. Her lips are spread wide over too large teeth. Her huge brown eyes are crinkled by laughter. At first I think it's a picture of a younger me, until I turn it over… 'Riley 2017' is written in black ink on the back. My heart leaps into my throat. Why would Hadley have a picture of my daughter?

CHAPTER EIGHT

I am sitting on the couch staring at Riley's picture when Hadley walks in.

"Aria? What are you still doing up?"

I glance at the clock. It's a quarter to midnight. It really doesn't feel that late.

"Did you clean?" Hadley asks in mock astonishment. She drops her bag by the door.

I nod. She still hasn't noticed the picture in my hand, but she does catch that I'm not speaking.

"What's wrong? Did something else happen?" Her eyes finally flick to my hands.

"Where did you get this?" I hold it out to her and her face contorts painfully.

"Where did you find that?"

"Hadley." I growl hot tears start burning my eyes. I hate that being angry makes me cry.

"I got it in the mail a couple months ago."

I shake my head at her. "What gives you the right?"

"The envelope was addressed to me. They asked me to show you if I thought you could handle it. But I *couldn't* Aria!" Her eyes are also wet with tears. "With everything you had going on it would have killed you."

45

The tears have finally made their way out and I attempt to blink them away. "Still, she's MY daughter. I have a right to hear from her, to see her." The couple said they would keep an open adoption even though I told them it wasn't necessary. At the time I imagined it being easier not seeing her grow up without me. It probably would have been. Ignorance is bliss.

"Aria, I did this to protect you. Can you really be mad at me for that?"

"What else did they send?"

"Aria…" She says softly.

"What else did they send!" I yell at her.

She huffs a breath at me. "A letter, the one they wrote to me, but it's gone. I threw it away." She admits quietly.

"What did it say?"

Hadley sighs. "She asked about you. Wanted to know where her mother was. They asked for a picture of you so Riley could keep you close to her. And they thanked you, endlessly, for giving them that perfect little girl."

Tears start streaming down my red cheeks. "Did you send anything back?"

"I sent them that picture of you pregnant. The one mom took where you're sitting on the swings in our backyard. I thought they'd like that. Seeing the two of you together."

I nod palming my face roughly to combat the tears. Hadley comes over and wraps her arms around me. That's when I break down completely, sobbing heavily into Hadley's shoulder. "I miss them so much."

"I know." She coos.

"Why did he do this to us? How could he just leave me like that?"

"I'm so sorry Aria, I'm sorry for everything."

I end up sobbing until I pass out from exhaustion.

I wake up startled and confused. All of the lights have been turned off, I can barely make out the shadowy figures of furniture around the room. I'm laying on the couch wrapped in one of our blankets. I throw it off of me and stand, stumbling through the living room to turn the hall light on. I slowly make it into bed, but when I try to sleep again all I can manage is to reach that place of delusion between wake and sleep. Like I'm watching a camera reel of images fly through my mind.

Tick* Riley is on the swings my father built.

Tick* James is standing in the yard with me watching her.

Tick* James grabs my hand. Kisses my cheek.

Tick* Riley runs toward us.

Tick* Clunk* The loud noise makes my eyes shoot open rousing me from my half sleep. I look around panicked, afraid Annette has found her way into my room again, but I only see darkness. I turn my bedside lamp on, banishing the creeping shadows back to their hiding places. Still nothing. Maybe I imagined the noise all together? I look over the lamp out the window next to my bed. I can see the few trees on our street swaying violently in the wind. November always brings storms with it. As I look down I can see the outline of a body. It raises a hand to me, green eyes burning out from the darkness. I stand up suddenly knocking the lamp and several other things off my bedside table. I claw the window open and the figure shoots toward me. Instinctively I duck and he lands on his feet on the other side of me barely making a sound.

47

"James." I cry and cling to him. I kiss his chest then throat then chin finally making my way to his mouth in the dark. I dig my nails into his shirt, all of me wanting to be near him at once. He is gentle with me. Holding my face as if it were porcelain even though I'm still clawing to get him closer to me.

"What are you doing here? Annette-"

"I can't stay away from you, it's impossible."

I smash my lips against his again. "James, I am so sorry." I whisper against him.

"Aria." He pulls his face away from mine and my heart races with panic. I'm still clinging to him, unwilling to let him go. "This isn't your fault. I sought you out."

"You can't be here." I whisper forcing my hands to my sides, my heart breaking as his hands also fall away from me.

"I know" He breaths. His eyes search my face for a moment. "Aria, do you know how long I've been alive?"

I shake my head confused at the direction he's taking.

"I was born in 1785."

"200 years?" The number doesn't make sense to me.

"I'll be 232 in April."

I look at his stone colored skin, his bright green eyes. "How?" He doesn't look a day over 25.

"Aria." I'm still amazed by how much I love hearing him say my name. A siren song. "Annette has given me an ultimatum." My stomach clenches. Here it comes. "Either I leave without saying goodbye, or I do and she kills me."

I grip his arm firmly, suddenly afraid of what else might shoot through my window tonight.

"Don't worry, she won't come tonight." He manages a smile. "I choose to see you one last time."

"What do you mean? If we run…"

"She'll find me, like I told you she always finds me."

I shake my head. I don't want to hear this. "I don't understand."

"He's going to kill himself." A voice says from behind me. I whirl around to find another vampire, one I've never seen before. He's tall and far too skinny for his height. His blue eyes and pale skin are too contrasted against his dark hair.

"Eric." James hisses.

"Who is this? What is he talking about?" I shriek.

"This is Eric, my… Brother." James replies hesitantly.

"I'm his creation." Eric corrects with a smirk.

I turned stunned to look back at James. "You're a creator? Why wouldn't you tell me that? Where has he been all this time?"

"Aria I *was* going to tell you. There have been more severe matters to deal with than telling you my life story."

"Yet you had no problem dragging up mine." I retort.

"He left me in Olympic National Park." Eric answers my question ignoring our tiff.

"Olympic Park?" I repeat.

"We've been living there for years trying to hunt and live off of animals in the woods instead of feeding on humans." James says.

"Quite the failed experiment." Eric scoffs. "You're looking well fed James."

I now realize why Eric looks so skinny.

"Stop it." James warns him. "I was at the house in Seattle grabbing us more supplies when I smelled her." I feel him stiffen beside me. "You know the draw of the enchanted

49

Moura. And then…" His eyes flick to my face. "Then I saw her, I couldn't… I couldn't leave."

"Well, here you are ready to die for her."

"Why do you keep saying that? James what is he talking about?" I'm so confused by all this new information I could scream.

"Have you ever heard of the term 'taming the sun'?" James asks.

"No." I shake my head. "What does that mean?"

"It means when the sun comes up, I'll be there waiting for it. Then this whole mess will be over."

"For you." Eric states. "For those of us who don't burst into flame, the mess will still be here."

James gives him a scolding look. "This is the only way."

Eric growls pacing the back wall of my room shaking his head as if they've had this conversation many times and there is no changing his mind.

"Aria." James tries to take my hand but I pull it away.

"You are going to kill yourself."

"Don't look at it that way." He says agitated.

"How am I supposed to look it it? That's exactly what you're doing."

"Two hundred years, Aria." He says grabbing me by the shoulders. "People aren't supposed to live that long. I'm so tired."

"And what about me?" I mumble. "You said when you spend centuries trying to find someone to share your life with you take the chance."

He looks down at me his eyes morose. "I would have spent forever with you. But I can't live without you, and I won't let Annette end your life. This is my only option, it's the best for all of us."

Eric growls again. "This is ridiculous."

"Eric, so help me-"

"You're sacrificing yourself for this pathetic human! We shouldn't even be here. James," He pleads. "If we leave now and don't look back, Annette won't waste her time trying to find a lost cause."

"Yes, she will. And she'll kill Aria before searching for me." He shakes his head. "I can't live without her."

"You CAN but you WON'T!"

"I would rather die!" James bellows back.

"Stop." I say. They both turn to look down at me. "Eric is right." I take James's hand. "I don't want you to go, but I would rather you be alive and without me than dead."

Eric gestures his hands at me, making an I-told-you-so face at James expectantly.

James sighs. "Can Aria and I have a moment alone, please?"

Eric shakes his head in defeat. "Fine, I'll be outside waiting." He walks to the window.

"No matter what I decide?"

Eric sighs, then nods slowly before disappearing through the window.

"Go with him." I plead. Either way his loss will be the death of me, but I don't want him to give up his life for me. My only hope will be Annette comes for me quickly.

"You're not listening." He puts his stone hands on either side of my face. "If I leave here without you I won't survive. This way I choose my own fate. Can you respect that?"

I don't speak. I only close my eyes and wrap my arms around him. We only have an hour or so before sunrise. He holds me back, kissing me slowly. That is how we spend our last minutes together.

"I'll go with you." I whisper as he stands to leave.

He shakes his head. "I don't want you to see it. I'll send Eric back here when it's over. I know you have a lot to ask him." He kisses me one last time then disappears out the window.

CHAPTER NINE

It seems like days before darkness finally falls again, but Eric never comes. I don't really know what to think about that. Obviously he doesn't care for me, still I was hoping he would give me a little sympathy considering we are in the same boat. I spend days curled up in my bed. At first Hadley came in every couple of hours to try to talk to me. She said she heard the yelling the night James left but didn't understand most of it. When she finally came to terms that I wasn't going to respond she gave up. Now, she only comes once a day to bring me a meal I almost never eat.

"Aria." She puts her hand on the small of my back. I roll over to look at her. "It's Sunday." She says softly. "I brought you some soup. I figured you might be cold. Have you looked outside?" Her eyes flick toward the window. "It's snowing."

I sit up to look out the window with her. My muscles are sore from lack of movement.

Hadley stares at me alarmed for a minute then relaxes when she realizes that's all I'll do for the day. "I called your work." She says. "Told them there was a death in the family."

I nod my head slowly in response, still mesmerized by the snow.

Our street is coated in white. Thick fluffy snowflakes are floating down from a clouded sky. It hurts to look at the spot where James once stood so I turn back only to find that Hadley is gone. I get up slowly and go through the motions of showering. When I finish I get dressed, then sit on my bed not knowing what to do next.

I'm still so angry at Annette for bringing me here, at James for making me care about him more than I care about myself, and at Eric, I hate him with everything in me. What horrible person would let me go through this alone? What kind of vampire disobeys their creators final wishes? I hate him for being able to know James in some ways I could never know him. I hate him for disregarding me so easily, for not even trying to trust me in even the smallest way.

I push my balled up fists into my eyes, trying to cram the tears back in. All I want is to be numb again. I would give everything not to have the pain of memories anymore.

That's when it strikes me. An idea so dangerous it will get me killed, but at this point, what other options do I have?

I grab my purse off the bedroom floor and run out the front door. When I hit the bottom of our steps I stop. This is too reckless. I turn back to look at our little apartment. The sky has once again turned grey leaving us in shadow. It's going to rain soon, this quiet blanket of snow will be washed away. Maybe it won't get me killed. Maybe Hadley and I can go back and we can fix me together. I should tell her where I'm going. I look at the snow under my feet. No. She'll talk me out of it. So, once again, I turn away from my home and head to their leir.

I trudge through the snow trying to pick my steps carefully. The sky is growing darker, any minute now the sun will sink behind the trees. I march on, it is silent except for my feet crunching through the ice, and my shaky breathing. I really should have grabbed another coat.

"Aria." A voice calls from my left.

Bewildered I turn to see Eric walking out of the dark trees towards me. I go to take a step back and slip on a patch of ice, right before I hit the pavement a hand grips my upper arm pulling me back up.

"Eric." I hiss through chattering teeth. I yank my arm from his grasp so I can continue walking.

"What are you doing?"

"What does it look like?" I snap dodging another ice patch as he glides right over it.

He sighs impatiently. "I know where you're going."

I stay silent. He may know where I'm headed, but he has no idea what I'm planning to do when I get there.

"What are you planning to do?" He asks.

I look sideways at him, once again suspicious that vampires can read minds.

"Do you really think Annette is going to let you crawl back to Perrous?"

I stop in my tracks turning to glare at him. "How could you think I would go back to Perrous?"

He shrugs looking down at me.

I turn and keep walking. "Go home Eric."

"Just tell me what you're going to do." He says taking a stride to keep pace with me. "You want Annette to murder you? Why? Because you think if you can't be with him in life you can be with him in death? I've got news for you kid, vampires don't get into heaven. We are soulless before death."

I give him a short humorless laugh. "I'm not killing myself." Not technically anyway.

He huffs a breath at me out of obvious conclusions. He is silent for a long minute. I would think he has left if I didn't know just how stubborn he is. Suddenly he takes my hand, so gently and with eyes so pained that all I can do is stop and stare at him in baffled confusion.

"Just tell me Aria."

The way he's looking at me makes me squirm. "Why do you care so much?"

He lets my hand slip away from his and takes a step back. The hard look snaps back into place. "I don't." He states.

I roll my eyes feeling stupid that I believed even for a second that he actually cares what happens to me. I keep walking.

"I made a promise okay?" Once again effortlessly keeping pace with me. "I promised James I'd keep you safe, and alive." He moves to stand in front of me blocking my path. "And dammit I'm going to keep that promise."

"Move." I press my hands against his chest to shove him, but it's like trying to shove a cliff face, he doesn't even waiver. I glare up at him. "Do you realize how ridiculous you sound? You are hell bent on hating me, but also on keeping me safe?"

He growls shaking his head. "I don't-"

"Yes, you do. I'm just not entirely sure why."

The hardness in his face lifts again. "Do you realize how heartbreaking it was to have James run off? To leave behind everything we were working toward, to leave me behind, for some girl? Yes, I hate you. James was the only family I've ever had. He was my best friend, my brother. You stole him from me, and now we'll both never see him again, because of you." His words are sharp and quiet.

I take a step back. Every word is like a bullet. I know now, more than ever that I'm making the right choice going to Annette. "He was my everything too Eric. You got a decade, I got a month." I look back up at him. Surprisingly he doesn't look angry. "I am so sorry for the pain that I've caused you. Let me fix it. Let me go now and you will never have to worry or care about me again."

"I made a promise."

"You also promised to come back for me that night. We wouldn't want you to start living up to my expectations." I offer him a weak smile but he continues to look at me with question.

I turn.

"Aria."

"Just, leave me alone Eric." I retort over my shoulder.

He stays, watching me walk away.

I knock on the enormous wooden door before me. The lump in my throat grows at I wait. The door finally swings open.

"Well well." Titus clucks.

I see Perrous freeze at the sight of me. Eyes wide like a doe caught in a beam of light.

"Your girl is back." Titus flashes his teeth his eye never leaving me.

Suddenly I'm being yanked through the open door. Titus has been thrown sideways and a small but strong hand has me by the hair. The door slams closed.

"I told you what would happen if you ever came back here." Annette hisses in my ear.

"Annette don't!" Perrous takes an involuntary step forward then freezes again when she turns to glare at him.

"I'm not here for Perrous." I say quickly watching the hope drain from Perrous's eyes. "I'm here to talk to you."

"And talk we shall." In a flash she releases her grip on my hair and grabs me by the arm, pulling me up the stairs and into the first door on the left.

"Start talking." She growls.

Terror is ripping through me, somehow I manage to form shakey words. "I'm wagering you a trade."

She laughs heartily. "Why on earth would I agree to that?"

"Because you want me out of the way."

She thinks for a minute, then walks towards me smiling. I freeze, not even daring to breath. She reaches out taking a lock of my hair, she twirls it around her bony finger. "What kind of trade?"

I repel the urge to smack her hand away from me. "You need a steady flow of blood. The others go out to hunt, but as the leader of a coven you are better than that. You should not be subjected to such an archaic way of life." I smile as slyly as I can muster.

She takes her hand back. "I'm listening."

"What if I can give you a reliable source of live bodies, every day if you wanted."

She narrows her eyes at me skeptically. "How would you manage to do that?"

"The restaurant where I work. I direct some bimbo and her boyfriend to the 'bathroom', where they will really come out in the alley beside the building. You send one of your... creations, to go snag them up and bring them to you. Mess free."

She smiles. "They always taste better when they're scared."

Sickeningly, I remember Perrous saying the same thing the night we met. I was terrified. "It's the adrenaline."

She looks at me her smile widening. "You are the most interesting human I have ever met. No wonder they are so drawn to you. Enchanted Moura indeed." She studies my face.

I remember James using that same expression. "What is that?" I blert, my fascination overtaking the icy hand that has clenched itself around my stomach.

Her cat like eyes blink at me. "The enchanted Moura are a Spanish myth, a fairytale. Much like the Greek Siren, the Moura are beautiful maidens who lure men in with promises of treasure. There is nothing like the call of the enchanted Moura, it cannot be ignored." She pauses for a minute lost in thought.

"And you think I'm one of them?"

"No." That horrible smile splits across her face again. "You're just a girl." She continues to smile at me for a moment then frowns. "This trade, what do you want out of all this?"

I take a ragged breath. "I want you to let me forget."

"Forget." She repeats, her eyes automatically flick to the door, behind which I bet Perrous is lurking.

I nod. "Forget Perrous, forget James." Saying his name makes my heart collapse. "All of it."

"And you believe I have the power to do that?"

Her eyes are searing, I have to look at the floor to escape them. "I know the effects of vampire venom." Better than anyone. "You are the oldest vampire in the state, and by far the most powerful. If there is anyone who could do this, it's you."

She smiles again. "You are right about that." She turns and walks to her dresser at the far end of the room, and opens a drawer. She walks back to me holding out a container. There are only two pills in it, she's done this before. "These are liquid capsules filled with my venom. In small doses, like when a person is bitten, it will make them forget the night. In large doses, like these pills, it will make the months slip away."

I take the bottle and hold it up to the light. The pills are iridescent red.

"These two pills will make you forget the entire year. Back to the day you met Perrous," She shrugs, "Except you won't. Move on with your life Aria. With a bit of my help you will survive."

"We have a deal then?

She nods. "Take those tonight and I will arrange to meet you tomorrow. As long as you keep up your end I won't kill you."

Bile rises to the back of my throat, so all I can do is nod.

I turn the pills over and over in my hand. I debate with myself for about the hundredth time. Do I really want to do this? Can I? Then flipping back to, yes. I have to. It is already midnight. I have to do it now. I roll them once again between my fingers before taking them both at once. I lay down, staring at my ceiling fan. I'm not tired. Too impatient and too hopeful of what the pills will take away. A pain begins to build in my head, within 15 minutes the aching is so strong I have to physically hold my head in my hands to keep the throbbing at bay, it is a pain so consuming that it eventually knocks me out.

When I awake, I'm doomed to live another day. I walk out into the kitchen to get coffee and Hadley gives me her signature worried stare.

"What?" I ask catching her watching me.

"Nothing." She glances away quickly. "I just… Are you okay?"

I assume she means in general. How am I coping with not seeing Riley? Or not seeing our parents, who shunned us both when I gave her up. She knows I'm not okay. I know she's not okay. So I nod. "It's not your job to worry about me."

She frowns.

"Hadley-"

"You seem different." She interrupts staring at me again.

"In what way?"

She looks me over with her sharp eyes. "I don't know. You seem better, somehow." She shakes her head. "After what happened -"

"I don't want to talk about what happened. It's over… Can we just let it be over?"

Hadley is still frowning but nods in agreement. I see her move uncomfortably out of the corner of my eye and my eyes click to hers. She's still staring at me, like she thinks I might spontaneously combust.

"I'm going out." I say slowly. I have no idea where I'll go but if I stay here with her watching me I'll scream.

She shifts again in her seat nodding.

I tie each shoe deliberately tight so I won't have to stop and retie them later.

I walk down Capitol Hill towards the waterfront, there is a park just past the train tracks Hadley and I used to visit when we were kids. I stay there staring out at the water until sunset. It's funny how time seems to flow faster in certain situations, then drags on in others. I try to make my walk back up the hill drag on, I don't want to get home early enough to have to try and make small talk with Hadley. I'm too exhausted for that. I decide to stop by the restaurant where I work, feigning confusion about what time I'm supposed to be in tomorrow. As I pass by the alley next to the restaurant I spot a dark figure lurking under a security light. I stop, a deer caught in headlights. Something about this image is so familiar I can't help but stare, just waiting for the memory to connect. The figure rushes at me in a gust of wind. Before I can comprehend what's happening we are on the roof. "Hello." The man breaths at me. He has both my hands locked iron tight in one of his, the other is holding my chin at an angle toward the sky. He puts his nose to my throat. "Oh God." I squeak. He rakes his fangs against my skin. "I've wanted to do this for too long." I scream as he bites down.

"Titus!" A woman's voice calls.

The man pulls away from me.

"What have I told you about attacking people in public." The woman yanks me out of his iron grip like she is breaking a paper chain. "Go home." She commands. "Now."

The man growls loudly before disappearing.

"Sorry, new vampires have very little control over their bloodlust."

I'm shaking at this point, and despite the venom running through me, my heart is going a mile a minute.

"Are you alright?" Her catlike eyes are searching me.

I can't speak so I nod quickly. I just want to get the hell out of here.

"My name is Annette. I am the creator of the Seattle coven."

"Aria." I reply still confused.

"Could I ask a favor of you, Aria?" She asks.

"Favor?" I squeak. What would she possibly want from me?

"Kitten, I just saved your life. So, yes, I would like to ask a favor."

"Okay." Even my voice is shaking.

"You work in this restaurant?" She inclines her head.

I nod slowly.

"I bet you get some patrons who drink far too much."

"A few." Please just let me be dreaming. I'm in bed right now, I'm in bed.

"So, you send them out into that alley down there." She points a boney finger. "And I make sure no vampire bothers you ever again."

I stare at the ledge of the building. "What will you do to them?"

The smile she gives me makes me sick. "Just... have a little fun."

"You can protect me from..." I look off into the dark sky. "That..."

She nods. "Yes."

A siren screams it's way down the block, making me jump. I stare down at my feet. "Okay. I'll do it. Whenever I have the chance."

"Let's say once a week, at least."

I nod again. "Fine." Just let this be over please.

She rushes me. "Let me get you home, I can't have you walking down the street like that."

I look down to find my shirt completely soaked in blood. I put my shaky hands up to it, trying to get it off of me. She stops me. "Just let me get you home, then you can freak out."

We shoot through the streets like a passing breeze in the night. Before I know it I am standing at the steps to my apartment. Annette is gone, and Hadley is staring at me from our open door in shock. "Aria, what happened?" She pulls me inside.

My head feels like it's vibrating, trying to find words is like trying to speak another language. "Vampire." Is all I can say.

CHAPTER TEN

For the next month I throw myself into endless activity. Keeping my mind and body busy is the only way I can survive. So I immerse myself in work. I spend at least 40 hours a week at the restaurant taking on additional shifts until Partick has to forcibly send me home. Even then I hardly spend any time at the apartment, only to sleep. When I'm not working or sleeping I'm walking. I wander all over Seattle, trying to become hopelessly lost so I can find my way back to something familiar. This goes on and on, for days that turn into weeks.

It's late and pouring down rain. I had taken it upon myself to scrub the entire kitchen. I'm elbow deep in soapy dishes when there is a knock at the door. Hadley is on the couch watching some insipid reality show. We swap a glance before I pull the door open. A very tall young man is standing in front of me. He is sickly skinny, but I can tell by the way he holds himself he is deceptively powerful.

"Hey." He pushes past me into our living room. I'm so shocked I don't even try to stop him.

"Eric." Hadley says suddenly sitting up. Does she have a new boyfriend I don't know about?

Eric turns to look at me his blue eyes are intense against his white skin. "I've been trying to get ahold of you for a month Aria." He growls. "Where have you been?"

"I told you she's hardly home, even to sleep." Hadley replies fussing with her hair.

"I'm sorry, who are you?" I ask.

They both stare at me blankly for a minute. "What do you mean?" Eric says.

"I mean I've never seen you before in my life." I look around him at Hadley. "Who is this?" Then back at him. "How do you know my name?"

Hadley looks at me in shock, and Eric doesn't answer me even though I'm still staring at him expectantly.

"He… He's a vampire Aria. He told me he was a friend." Hadley says.

"I never used the word friend." Eric mutters impatiently. "Aria" He reaches out to touch my arm but I pull back.

"I don't know you."

The man starts to pace our living room muttering under his breath. Then he looks at me suddenly. "What do you remember?"

"A lot of things." I reply annoyed.

He shakes his head equally annoyed. "Have you ever met another vampire?"

"Yea, I help out the leader of the Seattle coven."

He stops pacing. "Annette?"

I nod.

"Helping her?"

"Yes." I state impatiently. I can't explain why but I am extremely irritated by Eric's presents. I don't like the way he looks at me.

"Why?" He barks at me.

"I owe her a favor from a while back, why do you care about this?"

Realization falls over his stone like features, he shakes his head at me again. "Aria, you didn't?"

"Didn't what?" Hadley asks.

"I knew you were desperate, but I never thought you would result to that."

"What?" Hadley demands.

"She doesn't remember." Eric says. "Perrous, me, James, any of it…"

"How is that possible?"

"Annette must have erased her memory."

"She can't just do that!" Hadley shrieks.

"She's almost a thousand years old. She can pretty much do whatever she wants." Eric mutters.

"Will you two please stop talking about me like I can't hear you! Tell me what the fuck is going on!" I demand.

Hadley looks at me. "You don't remember James?"

"I…" I shake my head the name has no meaning. "No."

"Perrous?"

"No."

"Riley?" She can barely say it.

"Of course I remember Riley."

She releases a breath nodding.

"Aria, sit down." Eric demands.

I shoot him a glare but I can see the immediate regret at his tone. "Please."

So I sit there on our couch as they explain the last year of my life. If I think about it, it makes sense. This is why I feel like there is an empty part inside me. At first I thought it was all about losing Riley, about Daniel's suicide, but even that didn't explain why it felt like I was missing something. Even though I will never fully get over having to give up my baby, I was past the point of grief long before I moved in with Hadley. Something else made me into this shell of a body I am now. It seems weird, but I thought knowing what was missing would make me feel better. When in reality putting a name to it just makes me feel even worse.

I get up to put my shoes on.

"Where are you going?" Eric looks at me alarmed.

"I don't know." I admit. Anywhere is better than here, in this house with this stranger.

"I'll go with you." Hadley starts to stand but I stop her.

"Honestly, I just want to be alone."

The hurt that reaches Hadley's face makes me want to hug her.

"I just need to think all of this over, okay?" I reassure her.

"You don't believe me?" Eric says frustrated.

"I don't know what I believe anymore." I mutter. I turn and walk out the door without a second glance. All I want is to get as far away from this situation as possible.

Unsurprisingly, it's still raining. I had left my jacket back at the house, but not to my dismay. The rain feels good on my exposed skin. It starts to sooth my irritation as I walk. I try endlessly to only focus on the sound of my footsteps, but my mind keeps wandering back to Eric's voice. Replaying words that keep eating at the edges of my sanity. "She doesn't remember. Perrous, me, James…" James, the name sounds simultaneously foreign and familiar. Like when you say a word too many times in a row and your brain can't remember what it means.

I try to picture a face, anything that might match the name rattling around my head. But I'm searching for a memory that isn't there, and I only end up giving myself a headache.

I don't know how long I walk, or how far, but eventually I notice the sky turning a deep purple. I glance at a street sign trying to figure out where I am, but it's still too dark to make out. I stop at a corner pondering, finally able to figure out I'm on first street. Suddenly I'm so absolutely exhausted I actually consider calling a cab. Then I realize I don't have a wallet. I have to go back eventually. I trun on my heel to go back the way I've come, and nearly have a stroke as I run face first into something so solid it knocks me off my feet.

"Oh God." The something has a voice, and it is bending over to help me stand. "I'm so sorry, are you alright?"

I look up into bright green eyes. "Not your fault, I should look where I'm going." My arms tingle where his ice cold hands touched my skin.

He smiles at me, making a small shiver run through me. His eyes seem to brighten as he looks over my dazed expression. He is beautiful, the most beautiful thing I've ever seen. He must be a vampire.

I tear my gaze away from his impossibly green eyes. "I should go. Sorry, again." But I can still feel him watching me. "What are you looking at?" I accuse softly.

"Sorry?"

I make the mistake of looking back up at him. His resounding smile nearly knocks me back onto the concrete.

"Do I know you?" Something about this moment, about the way he looks at me, the way his lips curl over his sharp teeth, makes me think I've been here before. I have the strongest urge to reach out and brush my fingers over his cool skin. I clench my fists, pinning my arms to my sides.

The life drains from his face as he frowns. He continues to look me over. "No, you don't know me." He turns suddenly taking off down the street.

I stand frozen with shock as I watch him leave. Just like that he's gone. His smile, his eyes, they are only a memory.

I slowly walk back to the apartment in a trance. When I open the door both Eric and Hadley are waiting, staring at me expectantly once again.

"I need a drink." I head for the kitchen.

"It's like 6 in the morning." Eric says, as they follow me.

I crack a beer and hand it to Hadley. She downs it gratefully. I open another and hold it out to Eric, then pause feeling embarrassed. "Oh, right." I put the bottle to my lips taking a few chugs before acknowledging that Eric is still watching me.

"Aria, are you okay?" He asks.

No, I am far from okay. Yet surprisingly calm, maybe this has pushed me over the edge into completely dead inside. "I'm fine Eric."

Hadley finishes her beer. "I should go to sleep." She states giving me a look. Her eyes flick between myself and Eric.

"I'll talk to you later." I reply pretending not to notice.

She disappears around the corner to her bedroom.

There is an unpleasant pause as I finish my beer. My empty stomach soaks up the alcohol quickly, and I feel it's effects immediately.

"So," I say breaking the silence. "You and I... We're friends?"

He smiles smugly. "You could say that, yes."

"And James, you knew him too?" I ask.

Eric nods slowly.

"You loved him?" I say so quietly I hope he doesn't hear it.

He sighs. "You have to understand, he was my creator. He was everything, my only family."

"And mine too?"

He nods, again eyeing me carefully.

"He sacrificed himself for us?"

"For you." Eric snaps glancing away from me agitated.

"Right." I say in a small voice. "It was because of me." I sigh, sure that I've said this a thousand times, but I do it anyway because I need him to know it. "I'm so sorry."

He looks back at me. "Don't be." It seems like he means it. "Aria..." I see something flicker behind his eyes. "*I* am sorry."

I stare at him unfathomably. "What for?"

"I'm sorry that I couldn't see what James saw in you until now." He swallows. "You, Aria, are important. I'm sorry it took this much for me to realize that. I'm sorry, I couldn't keep my promises."

I blush at how intimate our conversation has turned, and I can't explain why but it sends a pang through my chest. Guilt, I realize after a moment.

Eric shifts uncomfortably at my silence.

"You've been here all night?" I ask to break it.

"I couldn't..." He pauses composing his expression and his next words. "I couldn't leave Hadley until I knew you were back."

I nod smiling silently to myself. "You should feed, you must be hungry." I say.

He looks to the door. "You're right, and it's late. You should sleep."

The smile melts from my face. How will I ever sleep? So many things for my mind to linger on. My eyes flick back to Eric, going places it shouldn't. I'm afraid if he leaves I'll be left in the darkness forever, by myself. The thought sends me into panic. "Could you stay?"

He looks at me eyebrows pinched. "I… would, but I really should feed."

"Luckily, I've got about 8 pints right here." I attempt a coy smile.

"Aria." He says my name slowly.

"Please," I resort to begging, I can't have him leave. "I don't want to be alone… I… I can't. This is the only way I can sleep. Besides I owe you, for telling me what happened."

He flinches at something I've said, but recovers so quickly I don't question it. "You don't owe me anything, and you are not alone, you have Hadley."

I nod slowly, we both know it's not the same.

"Eric, please. Let me do this for you." I look away from him ashamed. I realize I'm being incredibly selfish, that I'm leading him on, but I can't help it. "I need the venom. Please don't leave me here in my own head."

He shakes his head. "You do not know what you ask of me."

He is right, I don't know what effect this will have on me, only what I've heard others say. I shudder as a flash of the face of the vampire who attacked me flies into my head. It will be a miracle if he doesn't try to kill me. I swallow back the fear and grab one of his frozen hands. I lead him down the hallway to my bed. I sit and watch as he stands in front of me. He is handsome, his features sharp but elegant. The mask he has held on his face since walking into my home has fallen. Eric slowly raises both our hands, he carefully runs the back of my hand across his lips.

I try to suppress the shiver that works it's way down into my stomach.

He takes my hand in both of his. "Are you sure?" he asks his eyes flickering first to my face then back to my arm.

"Do it." I dare him.

He rakes his fangs over his bottom lip in hesitation. As if he was still deciding.

"Please."

Suddenly his mouth is open, fangs drawn. He strikes the flesh just below the hollow of my elbow. I gasp in a breath, it's as if someone is sticking me with dull needles. And then a haze gradually descends over my body. The pull of sleep slips over me and I fall under its spell.

"Thank you." Are the last words on my lips as I fall into a deep dreamless sleep.

CHAPTER ELEVEN

When I wake up Eric is gone, light is spilling in through the windows. I'm sure I was supposed to be at work today, but I can't seem to make myself care enough to call in. I hide out in my room for a few hours, until I know Hadley has left for work. I walk through the empty house trying to think of ways to occupy my thoughts. Eventually I land on doing what I always do, I wander. I walk to the only park near the apartment and weave myself in and around the trees. My thoughts keep falling back on the stranger I ran into last night. I keep picturing his green eyes searching my face. I continue to fantasize that we know each other, that he is here walking next to me with that smile playing on his perfect lips. Before I know it the light has begun to fade from the sky. I sigh knowing I'll have to make my way home soon. I don't think I can handle Hadley looking at me with her sad eyes. I need a plan to distract the both of us. So I plan something I know Hadley will go for.

"We should go out." I say watching her fold clothes.

"Out where?" She eyes me suspiciously.

"There is that new bar up the street."

Her eyebrows pinch together. "It's a gay bar."

"So? We'll go dance with some queens. It'll be fun."

She shrugs. "If you want."

We get dressed and head out of the house. I can't wait to be out of this silence. The only noise around us now is the clicking of our heels on the concrete sidewalk. We pass a pub on our way. The music spilling out catches Hadley's attention and she stops. "Why don't we just stay here?"

"Because this is definitely not a gay bar."

She smiles at me. "Is there something you need to tell me Aria?"

I roll my eyes at her. "I just don't feel like dealing with men tonight." My stomach squirms as Eric's face flashes through my mind.

"Then a gay bar is definitely not the place for us." Her smile widens as she pulls me towards the entrance.

God save me.

The place is absolutely packed. I have to elbow a few people to even reach the bar, and when we do Hadley has to shout our order at a young bartender. Her ponytail dancing behind her as she mixes our drinks. Hadley hands her money then hands me my drink. It's way too sugary, not something I would have ordered, but I'll take it if Hadley is buying. The crowd moves like water, a literal sea of people. I keep getting bumped from every angle, little splashes of my drink leap over the rim of the glass. I try to drink it as fast a possible, so I don't have to keep holding it. Hadley looks happy to be surrounded by all these people, but she keeps sneaking worried looks at me. After a few minutes of just standing there next to a table two younger guys approach Hadley. Not to my surprise, neither of them gives any intrest in me after Hadley's brief introduction. After about 30 minutes of listening to them drone on about all the clubs they've been to on Capitol Hill, I try to order another drink, but there is only the one girl behind the bar and much louder people keep catching her attention. I finally give up, noticing somehow Hadley has a new glass in her hand. I try to motion to her that I'm going to find the bathroom, but she is only half paying attention. I squeeze my way through to an opening by a wall. There is a hallway to my right but I can't see where it leads. I decide to take my chances, only to end up at the back exit. I push the door open and step out into an alleyway. There is a couple violently making out next to a dumpster. Unsurprisingly, I pass by them without any notice. The cluster of people standing out by the entrance are all shouting drunkenly at each other. Over the babble I hear someone shout my name. My heart leaps into my throat as I search for a familiar face. A tall red head is bobbing toward me. "Aria!" He says again.

"Hello." I say to be polite. I have no idea who this person is.

He continues to grin at me. "You don't remember me do you?"

I shake my head apologetically.

"Sure you do, we worked together briefly. I was a line cook, I'm Patrick's cousin."

"Charlie." I nod. His face does seem familiar now.

"It's good to see you again. You look great." His red hair is falling into his eyes, I wish he would push it aside, it's terribly distracting.

"Yea, thanks. I'm just here with my sister, she's inside."

"It's too crowded in there for me too." He is still grinning at me expectantly.

I have a bad feeling about this guy I can't put my finger on.

"Come on, I was just about to go in through the back. There are less people there."

Before I can protest he has his hand on my shoulder, steering me back toward the alley. My stomach does a flip as I realize the couple who was just standing here is gone, and I'm alone with this stranger. "I really don't think we can." I say quietly trying to shrug his hand off of me, but he grips the upper part of my arm pulling me along with him.

"I've done it a hundred times, trust me they don't mind."

Something in his voice makes me remember why I feel so uneasy about him. He was fired for harassing one of my waitresses. She told me how he would follow her into the back room, using any excuse, just so he could be alone with her. This time I plant my feet steadily so he has to stop.

"What's wrong?" He asks innocently.

"Nothing." He is gripping my arm tighter now, waiting for me to make a run for it. "I just want to stay out front." I try to keep my voice light, but it still comes out tinged with panic. I need to get away from him. There are no lights next to the building, no one can see us if they were looking from the street.

He keeps pulling me along with him. "Come on, I'm no vampire, I won't bite you." Even in the darkness I can see he is still grinning at me.

"Please stop." I try to replant my feet but he is much bigger than I am. He pushes me up against the concrete wall.

He grabs at me with his giant hands. "It's fine Aria. I saw the way you looked at me when we worked together." He has his wet mouth right against my ear.

I shove him as hard as I can but it only makes his hold on me tighter. "Stop!" I yell. The panic swells in my chest.

"Hey!" A voice calls from further down the alley.

He places one of his giant hands over my mouth so I can't scream, pinning me up against the wall with the other. "Fuck off dude, we're trying to be alone."

"I believe I heard the lady tell you to stop." The voice is closer now. I still can't see anything.

"I believe I told you to fuck off."

Suddenly Charlie's hands fly away from me, and I hear a loud thump as his body hits the opposite wall.

A cold arm reaches across me and we rush out the other side of the alleyway. We're walking too fast, I can barely keep my feet underneath me. "Are you alright?" The voice growls at me. We are finally under the lamp light so I can look up at his face. It's the stranger from my walk the other day. I would know those green eyes anywhere.

I can't seem to make words form so I only nod. I finally come to the realization that we are headed away from the bar. "Wait, my sister." I say with enough alarm that he looks down at me briefly.

"Hadley will be fine. I'm taking you home."

He's right, we are only a few blocks from the apartment, still she'll worry when she can't find me. Then it dawns on me I never said her name. I stay silent, and eventually my apartment building comes into view. I catch a glimpse up the stairs, and my heart nearly soars out of my chest when I see a figure standing by the doorway. "Eric!" I call to him. The cold arm around my shoulders does not fall.

"Aria." Eric is looking at the stranger next to me like he is on fire. "What happened?"

"I asked you to keep her safe, Eric. I told you, you need to watch her." The stranger hisses at him as I open the door.

"I *am* trying to keep her safe, what do you think I am doing here." Eric says.

"What *are* you doing here?" I ask looking at Eric. "And how do you know him?" I turn back to the stranger standing in my living room. "Who are you?"

His face flushes with anger. "No one you would remember." He growls.

My heart stops. I have the oddest sensation, like I'm falling from a great height. "James."

His sad eyes search my face, and again I have the strongest urge to brush my fingers against his skin.

"That's who this is, isn't it?"

"Aria…" Eric says softly.

"You told me he was dead!" I shout at him.

"Until a few days ago I thought he was. I saw him checking up on you."

I glare at James. "Why did you come back?"

"Because I'm foolish, that's why." He growls to himself. "I should have just let whatever happened happen."

Both Eric and I are silent. I have never been so torn between two emotions, I simultaneously want to kiss him and to punch him in the mouth.

"I had to let Annette think I had killed myself, which means I had to make everyone else think I had too. It was the only way to be sure she wouldn't come after you" James says quietly. He reaches out a hand, stroking my cheek with his cold fingers. "What did you do Aria?"

"I…" I can't speak with him looking at me like that.

"Somehow she got Annette to erase her memory." Eric says.

"Eric…" James says slowly, his eyes do not leave my face.

"Oh, yes, I suppose you want me to leave you alone now." I can practically hear him roll his eyes.

"I'm going to attempt to make Aria remember me so, yes, I think that would be wise."

I don't hear him leave, then again I'm not listening. James takes my face in his hands and puts his lips to mine. When he pulls away I have to gasp to catch my breath. Random pictures pop into my head, like looking back on a dream. I gasp again as I realize that they aren't dreams I am remembering, but actual events. Standing under a street lamp in an alley, staring at James's outstretched hand. The way it felt to run up those iron steps to the roof with him. I can see his house in my head, the both of us standing in it, and I can actually remember how his lips felt against mine the first time he kissed me.

"I missed you." He whispers.

"This will sound crazy, but I absolutely missed you too."

He smiles at me brightly.

"But what do we do now?"

"We do what she should have done in the first place." He presses his frozen mouth against my neck, causing me to gasp again.

"Oh? What's that?" I try to ask casually.

"I change you. Marry you." He smiles slyly. "We turn our backs on this place and never look back."

"James." I shake my head slowly. "We will have to spend the rest of our lives running."

"Yes, but-"

"And I don't want you to change me." I blurt out before he can finish his sentence.

He looks at me offended. "What?"

"I don't want to be a vampire. I'm sorry but it sounds awful. You would really wish upon me what you went through?"

He looks at me still confused. "No, of course not... I only... assumed." Finally he smiles again. "I want you to be human, to stay human." He corrects himself.

"And you really want to run around the country until I'm an old woman?"

His smile widens. "Yes."

I sigh tearing my eyes away from his. "I can't leave Hadley."

"Aria, Hadley is an adult, but she'll never grow up if she has to keep taking care of you." He takes my hand. "She will understand."

"And Eric? What is he going to do? Follow us around the country?"

"I quite thought you two were just starting to get along." His eyes flick to the inside hollow of my elbow, the spot where Eric bit me.

I cover it instinctively with my other hand. James only puts his cold hand over mine in response. "It's okay." He says quietly. "You did what you had to do to survive. I never should have put that on you."

"Still, I feel badly for manipulating him."

"Eric is young. He doesn't yet understand the difference between infatuation and love."

He removes his hand and continues talking normally. "Eric will stay here and watch over Hadley. That way you and I will both know our families are safe."

"It's not fair of us to ask him to do that, James. He wants to be with you."

He smiles to himself. "If I ask him to, he will stay. And he'll hate me for it, but it's what's best for him."

I smile back up at him. "Can we really do this?"

"As long as I have you I can do anything."

So I pack my life into one bag. I write Hadley a letter telling her not to worry, that I think it would be best for me to leave before I screw up her life too, I don't mention James or where we are going. As long as she doesn't have information Annette will leave her alone.

I finally wander back outside to find James standing next to a brand new black sedan. I don't ask where or how he got it. We are both silent as we speed out of the city. Annette will never believe I just left on my own, she will spend her last days trying to track us down, but right now as I look over at James's face, and out the window to watch the city lights fall away behind us, I don't care. My world my happiness and my life are finally sitting next to me again, and that is the only thing I will ever want.

James reaches over to take my hand, making me look back over at him. "Where would you like to go first?"

A huge grin blooms over my face. "Surprise me."

The end.